P9-CBD-700

This Book Belongs to

_____

For Josiah,
who knows the care and keeping
of mythical things

Copyright © 2014 by Emily Winfield Martin

All rights reserved. Published in the United States by Random House Children's Books,
a division of Random House LLC, a Penguin Random House Company, New York.

Random House and the colophon are registered trademarks of Random House LLC.

Visit us on the Web! randomhouse.com/kids

Educators and librarians, for a variety of teaching tools, visit us at RHTeachersLibrarians.com

Library of Congress Cataloging-in-Publication Data
Martin, Emily Winfield, author, illustrator.
Day dreamers / Emily Winfield Martin. — First edition.
pages cm.
Summary: "Scaled, horned, and feathered creatures are the mythical friends that carry children into their day dreams." —Provided by publisher.
ISBN 978-0-385-37670-9 (trade) — ISBN 978-0-375-97326-0 (lib. bdg.) — ISBN 978-0-375-98217-0 (ebook)
[I. Stories in rhyme. 2. Animals, Mythical—Fiction. 3. Imagination—Fiction.] I. Title.
PZ8.3.M41852Day 2014 [E]—dc23 2013048795

MANUFACTURED IN CHINA

10 9 8 7 6 5 4 3 2 1

First Edition

Day Dreamers

A Journey of Imagination

Emily Winfield Martin

Random House New York

They say there are no dragons left
And that's the way it seems.
To find them you must visit
The land of waking dreams.

You don't need to search for secret doors
Or magic words to speak.
Your imaginings will carry you

Anywhere you seek.

And the ordinary world
Will never guess where you have gone

To chase your wondering, wandering heart
Into the place beyond.

Or the beyond may come to you
Dressed up in a disguise.
Is it the wind that moves the clouds?

Or a dragon as he flies?

A tiny seaside kingdom
Might grow beneath your gaze . . .

As creatures ancient as the sea
Rise on enchanted waves.

In a place of hushed and quiet things . . .

You might hear a phoenix call.

Or in the pattering of raindrops . . .

Jack-a-loping paws may fall.

In a hall of stones and echoes
Around the corner's bend . . .

Two nimble-footed unicorns
Meet two brave-hearted friends.

So listen very closely
   As you read of all these things.
Is it the whispering of pages . . .

Or the sound of griffin wings?

And when you leave, you learn the thing
That all day dreamers learn:
When you leave the realm of magic beasts,
They wait for your return.